MULBERRY GROVE
THE RING

By
James L. Grant

Mulberry Grove
The Ring

Prologue

"Leave me!" the queen commanded
her servant. "Tell the guards to stand
watch at the door. I want no one to
enter until you hear my summons."

The servant bowed her head as she
knelt to the ground.

"As you wish, my queen."

The queen turned to face the
terrace as the servant exited the room.

"Remember," she said adamantly,
"no one is to enter until they hear my
call."

"It shall be so," the servant
replied.

Once the door closed, the queen
walked over to an elaborate marble

table. On top of the table rested a gold box. The box was studded with diamonds while one lone ruby adorned the elegantly decorated lid.

"The secrets of the ages shall be whispered in my ears," the queen said as she lifted the lid of the box. "I shall be queen forever."

The queen gently picked up a piece of cloth that lay in the center of the box. She held it close to her heart as she slowly walked onto the terrace. The outline of the great city of Cairo greeted her as she stood in the afternoon sun overlooking the majestic pyramids.

As she unwrapped the cloth, a ring sparkled in the sunlight. The queen lifted it into the air and watched as the yellow stone from its center reflected onto the floor.

"It is time," she whispered.

The queen placed the ring on her finger and closed her eyes. She listened intently for someone or something to speak to her. The only thing she could hear was the clamor of slaves working on the roadway below.

"I have failed," she thought. "The spirits have betrayed me."

Without warning, the floor began to tremble. The queen opened her eyes to find someone staring at her.

"It can't be!" she said in astonishment. "What manner of cruelty is this?"

Before her stood the ghostly figure of a man. He was wrapped in the cloth that was used to shroud the dead. His emaciated face could be seen through the shreds in the fabric.

"Foolish woman," the man moaned. "Your greed has overtaken you. Did you think you could disturb the dead without any consequence?"

The queen said nothing as she backed away from the specter.

"Did you?" he moaned again.

"I am the Queen of Egypt!" she roared. "You shall pay dearly for your insolence. Be gone or I will..."

The man smiled broadly and began to laugh.

"It is you that shall pay dearly," he bellowed.

With that, the ghost raised his hand and pointed toward the queen.

"Guards," she yelled loudly. "Come quickly!"

The guards pounded on the door but it wouldn't open. The queen tried to run but her feet were unable to move.

"You shall receive what you have asked for," the man continued. "For disturbing the dead, you shall forever walk among them. You shall become Queen of the Night."

The phantom waved his arm. In an instant, the queen dissolved into a pile of salt. Her crown, her jewelry, and her clothing fell onto the mound of crystals. Her ghostly figure arose like a phoenix from the ground. She walked toward the man and stood beside him.

"Come walk with me," he said as he

took her hand. "The priest should have warned you before you placed that ring on your finger."

The queen looked at him with a blank expression on her pale face.

"You have no heart," he continued. "And now you must suffer the consequence."

In an instant, they both vanished. The door to the queen's room burst open and the guards gathered inside. The only thing remaining was the pile of salt and the queen's belongings.

"Beware the ring," a voice called from the distance. "Let this be a lesson to those who wear it. Be possessed of heart, mind, and spirit if you are foolish enough to disturb where the living don't belong."

The guards put their hands over their ears as the room filled with laughter.

"I am still your queen," a woman's voice called out. "I am still your queen."

The voice grew softer and softer until it faded away completely.

"Pretty amazing," said Andrew Alexander as he closed the tattered book. "What a great story. Do you suppose a ring like that ever existed?"

The archeology professor got up from his desk and strolled over to Andrew. He took the fragile document and placed it back in its protective case.

"It's quite possible," he replied as he closed the seal on the case.

"Maybe someday you'll find out."

"Yes, maybe," laughed Andrew.

"Maybe."

Chapter 1

"Can anyone here tell me why the Egyptians mummified their dead?"

You could hear a pin drop in the classroom as the students stared at one another.

"Anyone can answer," the man replied. "Don't be shy."

The presenter, Mr. Alexander, stood motionless at the front of the room. He looked very serious in his matching three-piece suit and dark blue tie. His face, what could be seen from behind the thick red hair of his beard, was rugged and riddled with lines - lines drawn on the faces of middle-aged men. The red hair on the top of his head was flecked with gray and looked carefully groomed. His voice was gentle and soothing.

David, who was fidgeting in his chair, accidentally knocked his pencil and notebook onto the floor. The commotion broke the silence and all eyes in the classroom turned toward him. Without hesitation, David's best friend, Luke, began to snicker. Jennifer, who sat two seats behind Luke, cleared her throat and coughed, signaling Luke to be quiet.

As Mr. Alexander resumed speaking, he noticed a hand moving in the air. Janeen Davis, who sat in front of David and who had an answer for everything, cocked her head back proudly and waved her hand until she got Mr. Alexander's attention.

"Do you have a question for me?"

"No," replied Janeen. "I have an answer. The Egyptians mummified their dead because they wanted their bodies in the next world."

David quietly groaned to himself.

"That's right," replied Mr. Alexander. "Do you know why they took such care to create these great tombs for kings that contained their possessions as well as their mummified body?"

Janeen sat for a moment, deep in thought. "Didn't they think they would need their things to help them when they woke up in their next life."

"That's exactly right! They wanted to preserve their body and keep with them the things that would help them in their next life."

Mr. Alexander walked over to the desk at the front of the room and opened a big glass case. He took out a collection of objects and placed them on the desk. Pieces of jewelry and broken pottery were carefully set out for display.

Both David and Luke leaned forward in their desks to get a better look at the objects.

Mr. Alexander picked up a small gold ring from the desk and showed it to the classroom.

"A ring like this was found at an archeological dig in 1925. I think you'll find the story of how this ring was made to be very interesting."

He then went over to his briefcase and took out a large poster. He

carefully unfolded it and then held it
up beside the ring.

"You see these three symbols on
this poster. These symbols were
etched into the ring that was found at
the tomb of a great pharaoh. These
symbols represent the heart, the mind,
and the spirit. In my research on the
history of this ring, I discovered a
legend that had been handed down over
the centuries. It was said that this
ring was made by an Egyptian priest
for the queen of a pharaoh. The ring
was supposed to give the wearer, the
queen, the ability to communicate with
the dead. She was supposed to be able
to gain knowledge of the next world
from the dead. The heart, the mind,
and the spirit were all supposed to

help her to understand what the dead were saying to her. If she did not use all three of these things, she would not be able to communicate to the next world."

"Luke," David whispered, leaning across the aisle. "We've got to talk to this guy after class."

Luke nodded in agreement and then looked back at Jennifer and silently mouthed the same thing to her.

"The priest warned the queen," continued Mr. Alexander. "He told her that she may find lost souls and thieves who might lie to her and trick her. She would need her most powerful weapons to protect herself. Only her heart, mind, and spirit would lead her to the truth."

"Could anyone who wore the ring communicate with the dead?" asked Janeen.

"Well, I suppose so," replied Mr. Alexander. "The legend says it was made for the queen, but I've never read anything else about it. I've never found any stories of people who've used the ring. It's interesting to wonder."

"Have you ever tried it on to see if it worked?" she asked.

"Oh no, this ring is a replica of the ring that was found in 1925," he replied. "I had this made for myself from a picture of the real ring that I found over at the university. It looks just like it."

Mr. Alexander passed the ring

around so that the students could examine it in their hands. When the ring got to David, he couldn't stop looking at it. He held the ring up to the window beside him and watched as the sunlight reflected off the stone in its center, casting a brilliant yellow shadow on his desk.

Their teacher, Mrs.Perry, who had been standing at the side, walked to the front of the classroom as Mr. Alexander finished his presentation. She stood beside David and waited for him to give her the ring. David continued to stare at it, not noticing she was there. As he moved his finger along the symbols on the ring, he felt Mrs. Perry tap him on the shoulder. Embarrassed, David dropped the ring on

17

his desk. Mrs. Perry picked it up and then continued on her way.

"I would like to thank Mr. Alexander for being kind enough to share with us his knowledge of Egyptian artifacts," she said as she turned to face the classroom.

"As you know, this concludes our weeklong study of different civilizations. I hope that you've all enjoyed the presentations this week - and please remember to turn in your assignments before you leave the classroom."

Just then, the bell rang and Mrs. Perry got ready to dismiss the class for the day.

"One final thing," she said. "Mr. Alexander owns the two fine antique malls downtown and he also volunteers his time as an assistant in the archeology department at the university. If you have any questions about what you've heard today, I'm sure that he would be glad to hear from you. Class is dismissed."

Luke, David, and Jennifer collected their things and stood at Mrs. Perry's desk to watch Mr. Alexander put away the artifacts.

"I really enjoyed your presentation, Mr. Alexander," said Luke.

"Yeah, so did I," replied David. "Just between us, have you ever really talked with the dead?"

Both Luke and Jennifer turned toward David and glared at him.

"You'll have to excuse him," said Jennifer as she gently poked her finger into David's side. "He tends to speak first and think later."

"No, no, that's a very good question," replied Mr. Alexander. "I'd probably ask the same thing."

David looked over at Luke and Jennifer and smiled. He picked up the ring and again examined it in his hand.

"You know," he said as he twirled it around in his fingers, "I bet you this ring would let me talk to the dead."

"Come off it David," replied Luke in a condescending tone. "You can't possibly believe this ring would contact the dead."

"Sure I do," he replied. "It's possible."

"Television has warped your brain."

Mrs. Perry, who was still in the room, walked over to Luke and David.

"Well," she said. "Why don't you do some research on the ring yourselves?"

The three of them stood very still and didn't say a word.

"This might be an excellent way to learn more about the Egyptian culture."

They looked at one another waiting for someone to respond.

"I'll give you extra credit points," she said, focusing her eyes on David.

David got a sick feeling in his stomach. He hadn't been doing very well in her class and he knew he couldn't turn down extra credit.

"Just write me a short summary on the information you find at the university," continued Mrs. Perry.

They watched one another closely. No one wanted to commit to extra work.

Jennifer, who had been quiet during Luke and David's outburst, suddenly replied for all of them. "Sure," she said. "We'd love to." She then turned toward Luke and David.

"Wouldn't we?" she asked them with a quizzical look on her face.

Luke and David coldly stared back at her, not saying a word.

"Fine then," replied Mrs. Perry.

"I'll expect a short paper from each of you in a couple of weeks."

Mr. Alexander finished packing up his artifacts and began to walk out of the classroom.

Jennifer walked over to him just as he reached the doorway.

"Do you know anyone that could help us at the university?"

"I have a friend named Jean Lumore who works there," he replied. "He has a much greater knowledge of Egyptian artifacts than I do. His mother was born in Egypt and she's taught him about the Egyptian culture his entire life. I'm sure he'd be a great help to you if you need information on Egypt."

"I'm sure we could use it,"

23

replied Jennifer. "We're not really sure what we're going to look for."

Mr. Alexander then took his ring and handed it to Jennifer.

"Maybe you can start your research with this."

"What do you mean?" she asked.

"Well, you could try and find out any information you can about this ring."

David stood between them. "What a great idea."

"I'd love it if you could find any new information on it. Let me talk with Mr. Lumore and see if he would be able to help you get started."

Mrs. Perry began to escort Mr. Alexander outside. Just as they were about to turn the corner, Mr.

Alexander leaned back.

"I'll make sure Mr. Lumore will know you're coming to the university. He's there most afternoons and evenings so he's easy to find. Call me if you need my help in any way."

As soon as they left, Luke turned toward David.

"This is great," said Luke sarcastically. "We have to write a paper because you can't keep your imagination quiet."

"Don't start with me, Mr. A plus," David shot back.

Jennifer rolled her eyes. "All right, calm down you two. This just might turn out to be pretty cool."

"How do you figure?" asked Luke.

"Think of it this way," she said.

"Wouldn't your dad be impressed that you would go to the university to do research on a school paper?"

Not saying a word, Luke walked up to the chalkboard and, without realizing it, picked up the erasers. Quietly, he began to erase the board. He thought about what his father might say to him. In his mind, he could see his father sitting at his desk at home.

"Don't settle for mediocrity, Luke," he heard his father's voice say.

Since his mother's death, Luke relied on his father's approval. When his mother died, a part of Luke's father seemed to die with her. Luke's father bottled up all of the carefree, childlike feelings that his wife brought out of him. The only thing that seemed to comfort him was his work and achievements. He worked hard to become head of the English department. He drilled into Luke the importance of excellence and hard work.

Luke, finally noticing what he was doing, put the erasers down and stared at the chalkboard. He could see his mother's face. She loved to tell ghost stories and was fascinated by spirits. She would have told him to do the paper just for the fun of it. "Fun?" he thought. "This could be fun."

"All right," he replied. "I'll do it."

Luke then turned to David and pointed his finger at him.

"Don't be thinking that you're going to talk with any dead person, David. You always get this way. This is not an episode of...a...Secret...a...what's its name."

"Secrets of the Universe," David replied.

"Whatever, things like that only happen on television."

Luke walked over to the window, turning his back toward David.

"You mean to tell me that you don't want to talk with the dead?" asked David.

"No," said Luke as he turned around. "I mean to tell you that you're really gullible."

Jennifer stood between Luke and David.

"You know, this may sound stupid but wouldn't it be great to talk to someone from the past that you've never met?" she said. "I mean, someone from your family. I never met my grandfather, and I've always dreamed of speaking to him one day."

"Oh great," replied Luke. "David's rubbing off on you."

"Chill out. I was just daydreaming. Let's just go and do the paper and forget about speaking to the dead. Agreed?"

"Agreed," they both replied.

The three of them picked up their books and walked out of the classroom.

"How are we going to get to the university?" asked David, as they made their way down the corridor.

"My dad would be willing to take us with him when he teaches his evening class," replied Luke.

Jennifer slowed to a stop and turned toward Luke.

"What should we do with the ring until then?" she asked. "Do you want me to keep it?"

David quickly raised his right palm in front of Jennifer.

"I'll take it," he replied.

"Oh, no you won't," said Luke as he lowered David's hand. "I'll take it home with me tonight and keep it in a safe place."

Luke took the ring from Jennifer

and put it in his pocket.

"Let's meet tomorrow after school
and we'll go to the university with my
dad. We can go to the library while
he's teaching his class."

They all agreed as they walked out
of the school building. Just as Luke
and Jennifer were about to walk away,
David turned toward Luke and smiled.

"Don't forget to watch "Secrets of
the Universe," it's on at eight
o'clock."

Luke turned around, looked at
David, and rolled his eyes upward.

"I wouldn't dream of missing it,"
he replied sarcastically and continued
on his way.

Chapter 2

Luke turned toward the window on his left and stared out at the countryside as it passed by him. It was a beautiful afternoon. The sky was blue and everything seemed fresh and alive. He felt safe watching the world drift by from the back seat of his car.

Suddenly, Luke noticed something strange. The car he was in didn't seem familiar. He moved his hands along the seat but the texture didn't feel right. The seat was smooth and cold. He was expecting the soft, warm feel of cloth. He looked down at the seat and saw the sun reflect off of the cool black leather.

"Leather seats?" he thought. "My dad's car doesn't have leather seats."

Luke looked up and stared directly into the rearview mirror. It was as if he was staring at a painting. A pair of eyes was watching him but they belonged to someone else. A cold tingle ran through his body as goosebumps dotted his arms. It was someone else's face attached to his body.

"What the--," he thought to himself. "This is crazy."

He then turned his attention toward the front of the car and his eyes focused on the driver. His heartbeat began to race as he realized that he didn't recognize the person driving the car. Sweat began to roll down his forehead.

"This can't be happening," he said to himself.

No sooner had he spoken these words than the car began to swerve. He grabbed hold of the seat trying to brace himself. It was no use. The car was swerving back and forth so quickly that he lost his grip. He fell to the floor of the car, bruising his left hand as he landed. It felt like the car was going out of control and rolling down a steep hill. He tried to look out of one of the windows to see what was going on, but he was being tossed around so violently that he couldn't get his balance.

Suddenly, the car came to a crashing stop, hurling Luke across the seat. For a moment there was silence. Luke lifted himself up to see what had happened. He looked over the back of the driver's seat and could see that the driver was lying against the steering wheel unconscious. He wanted to get out of the car as quickly as possible. Luke tried to open the door, but it wouldn't budge. He moved over to the other car door, hoping it would open. His pulse raced as he kicked the door with his foot. Luke could hardly breath as he wiped the sweat from his eyes. His clothes were so wet from perspiration that they clung to his body.

"This car is going to explode," he thought. He could feel the blood rushing to his brain. His head felt as heavy as a ten-ton lead weight.

He tried to think of another way
out. Terror struck him as he realized
that he was trapped. He put his hands
up to break the window, but quickly
turned away as it was too hot to
touch. The car began to fill with
smoke. Luke couldn't see anything and
he found it harder to breath. He felt
as if he was going to die. At that
instant, he began to lose
consciousness.

As he closed his eyes, he felt
light as air. It was as if he floated
out of his body. He looked down and
he could see the body of a strange boy
lying unconscious in the car. Somehow
he knew the boy's name. He turned
away from the sight, only to find the

boy standing next to him. The boy
didn't say a word. He just stood
there looking at Luke.

The boy was holding a book in his
hand. He opened the book and showed
it to Luke. The book revealed a
newspaper clipping of the accident.
It had the names and dates of the
boy's life and it detailed the events
of the accident. Luke reached over to
turn the page of the book but he
couldn't grasp it. He began to fall.
Faster and faster he fell. Just as he
was going to hit the ground, he awoke
and sprang up in his bed. He was
dripping with sweat and his covers
were on the floor.

"It was a dream," he said. "It
was all a dream."

Luke looked down at his right hand and saw the ring Mr. Alexander had given them. He tried it on after he got home from school and had forgotten to take it off when he went to bed.

"I must be going crazy," he mumbled. "It was a dream, it had to be a dream. But it was so real."

He noticed that his left hand was swollen.

"How could that happen?" he thought. "It couldn't have been real. It's not possible."

Luke got up from bed and walked into the bathroom. He splashed his face with water and stared into the mirror.

"It's just not possible," he thought as he dried his face with a towel. "My imagination is playing tricks on me. That's it. Maybe David's right. Deep down inside I must want to believe the ring works."

Luke walked back to his room and sat on the bed. He could feel his left hand ache as he propped himself up with his pillow.

"How does that explain my hand?" he wondered. "I may be crazy but I'm taking this thing off."

Luke took the ring off of his finger and set it on his dresser. He laid back down and stared at it. He could see it sparkle from the moonlight hitting the yellow stone in its center. There was something eerie about the ring as it glowed in the darkness.

"I know David and Jennifer will
think I'm teasing them," he thought.
"When we go to the university
tomorrow, I'll look at the old
newspaper files and see if the
accident I dreamed about might really
have happened."

Luke rolled over and looked out
his window.

"What'll I do if it really
happened?" he wondered.

His mind was racing but he slowly
drifted back to sleep. The next day
at school, Luke didn't say a word
about what had happened the night
before. He waited until school was
over and then convinced Jennifer and
David to walk home with him. As they
reached the roundabout that lay in the

center of the small town, they stood
and waited for a clearing among the
cars so they could walk across the
street.

"I'll bet you guys will never
guess what happened to me last night,"
Luke said, not looking directly at
either David or Jennifer.

"What?" asked David as they began
to walk across the street. "You got in
a fight. I noticed you hurt your
hand."

"No, I think I spoke to someone,
...uh."

The traffic began to move again as
they made it to the other side of the
street. The noise from the car engines
was so loud that it muffled Luke's
voice.

"What did you just say?" asked Jennifer.

Luke hesitated and began to chew on his fingernails.

"Yeah, you spoke to someone. Who?" replied David.

"Now, I'm not really sure if it was...uh."

"What already?" replied David. "Spit it out."

"I think I experienced someone dying in a car crash and then I spoke to them after they were dead," Luke replied, barely taking a breath.

Jennifer looked over at David and rolled her eyes.

"Stop teasing him Luke. We know you don't believe you can speak to the dead. I thought we were past this."

"No, really, I'm not kidding," he said as he followed Jennifer and David on the sidewalk.

"Luke, you can stop already," replied David. "We're not that gullible."

Luke grabbed both Jennifer and David by the shoulder and forced them to stop walking.

"No, you don't understand," he insisted. "I'm really not kidding. There's something to this ring. I can't explain it, but this WAS NOT a dream."

David stared at Luke and watched the expression on his face as he talked.

"So what you're telling us is that you, the ultimate disbeliever, talked with the dead."

"That's what I'm telling you," replied Luke.

"Are you sure you weren't dreaming?" asked Jennifer. "I mean, yesterday you wouldn't even say the word 'dead' and now you're telling us you've spoken with them."

Luke pulled out a notebook from his backpack and opened it to a page he had written on.

"Look, I think there's a way to find out if it was a dream," he said as he turned the pages. "The boy who died showed me a newspaper clipping of the accident. I wrote down what I could remember from the article."

"Oh, a well-read spirit," teased David. "I guess there's no cable TV in the after life."

"Knock it off," replied Luke as he continued. "The article had details of the boy's life and the dates of his birth and death."

"So?" Jennifer replied.

"So, when we go to the university tonight, we can look at the old newspaper clippings to see if that boy really existed."

"I don't know Luke, this seems pretty far-fetched," replied Jennifer as she began to walk away. "We have to do research on Egypt for that paper."

"Forget the paper. We can whip something up for that," said Luke as he followed Jennifer. "We could really be onto something with this ring."

"That's just what I said yesterday," cried David.

They continued walking around the roundabout until they got to the sidewalk that branched off to Luke's street. They turned onto it and walked the five blocks to his house. Luke's neighborhood was part of the older section of town where a lot of the professors owned homes. The houses were built mostly in the 1920's and many of them had large front porches with wood trim that was carved with elaborate designs.

Luke's house sat back some distance from the sidewalk and was tucked under a beautiful old mulberry tree that drooped over the porch.

"My dad won't be ready to leave for class for a couple of hours yet," said Luke as he walked up the steps onto his porch. "We'll just go up to my room and wait until he's ready to leave."

Luke opened up the screen door and began to walk inside.

"Maybe we can get the ring to work again," said David.

Luke quickly shut the door, pushing Jennifer and David backwards.

"Don't talk like that around my father," he said as he took David aside. "You know how he gets. If he thought we were getting involved with the spirit world he'd flip out. I'd be treated to daily lectures on how to be more practical. No thanks. Just keep it between us, OK?"

"All right," replied David as he pushed Luke away. "Don't go ballistic on me."

They went into Luke's house and climbed up the stairs to his bedroom. Luke's father, who was changing his clothes for work, walked out of his bedroom and met them at the top of the stairs.

"Oh, Dad, do you mind if we go with you to class tonight?" asked Luke as he approached the top of the stairs. "We have a paper to do for school and our teacher said we might try using the university library."

"No, I don't mind," replied his father. "I think it would be a good learning experience for you three.

Just be ready to leave at 4:30, OK?"

"No problem," replied Luke.

"We'll study in my room 'til you're ready to go."

"Fine. I'll call for you when I'm ready to leave."

Chapter 3

Luke, David, and Jennifer said goodbye to Luke's dad and walked over to the university library. As they walked up the steps into the building, David looked over at one of the stone statues that sat on either side of the entryway.

"Isn't that creepy?" he asked.

"Isn't what creepy?" replied Jennifer.

"The eyes on that lion are following me."

"You're imagining things," Luke chimed in.

Luke then went over to the lion and placed his hand on its eyes.

"See," he said as he turned

around. "They're staring straight
ahead."

"They weren't a minute ago."

"Come on, let's go," said Luke as
he grabbed David's hand. "We've got
work to do."

The library was a forbidding
presence. It was built around the
turn of the century and, from the
outside, seemed as if it was stuck in
time. The large, gray stone building
appeared bleak and cold. Its inside
was a mixture of old and new. The
enormous oak desk in the lobby had
been there for decades. Computer
terminals and the modern-looking
elevator were the only clues that you
were still in the present. Everything
else seemed linked to the not-so-

distant past.

Luke, David, and Jennifer strolled past the desk and got in the elevator.

"Where are we going?" Jennifer asked. "Does anyone know what floor we're supposed to go to?"

"We're supposed to go to second floor," replied David.

"How do you know?" asked Luke.

"Trust me, I've been here before."

"Oh, right! When?"

"Trust Me."

They arrived at the second floor and stood in the hallway. A big sign on the wall pointed to the rooms located on that floor. One arrow on the sign pointed to a room filled with maps and the other pointed to a rare book room.

"Oh, this looks right," replied Luke sarcastically. "We're supposed to use the microfilm machines, not look at maps."

"So I made a mistake," said David. "It happens."

"It sure does," answered Luke. "A lot."

David and Luke began to push each other around playfully. Jennifer, ignoring them, walked over to an information desk she spotted down the hall. David and Luke were so involved in fooling around that they didn't notice they were making a commotion. In fact, they didn't even notice the student who was walking toward them.

"Hey, you kids," the student called. "This isn't a playground.

What are you doing up here anyway?"

Luke and David stopped in their tracks.

"We're sorry for making so much noise," said Jennifer as she made her way back to the boys. "We'll try to be more careful."

The student gave them an angry stare and then walked away.

"We're supposed to go to the third floor," said Jennifer. "I talked to the librarian down the hall, and she told me where to go and who to talk to to get help using the machines upstairs. You guys be quiet and follow me."

Luke raised his eyebrow at David and they both followed her lead. They went to the third floor and waited behind Jennifer as she got instructions on how to use the microfilm machines. They each put their things in a pile on the floor and gathered around a table.

"We have to find the back issues of 'The Chronicle,'" Luke said, trying to clear space in front of him. "Since it's the local paper, I'm sure they'll have copies of it."

Jennifer sat down next to him and began to examine his notebook.

"Do you know what year the accident happened?" she asked.

"I wrote down all of the details that I could remember," he replied. "Let's see, here it is. The accident happened here in Mulberry Grove in 1968. The boy's name was Josh Taylor and he was 10 years old. I don't remember what month the accident happened, but I do remember the article saying something about a spring thunderstorm."

"Well, that must mean we should start with the files for April and May," replied Jennifer. "David, go ask the clerk for the microfilm for those two months."

David walked over to the counter and soon returned with two boxes of microfilm.

"One for you," he said, handing the first box to Jennifer. "And one for you, Luke."

Jennifer and Luke each sat down at a reader and began to examine the microfilm. David looked over their

shoulders as they slowly scanned each
article for any mention of the
accident.

"I don't see anything here that
resembles the article I saw," said
Luke as he reached the end of his
reel.

"Wait!" exclaimed Jennifer. "I
think I've found something."

Luke stopped what he was doing and
leaned over to Jennifer's terminal.

"That's it!" he cried out.
"That's the article."

"Sshh," replied Jennifer. "Let me
read it."

Luke and David crowded behind her
as she read the article out loud.

"Luke, you were right. A boy
named Josh Taylor died in a car

accident over at Sumner's Crossing. He and the driver were killed as the car rolled off the edge of an embankment and caught fire. It also says the boy was placed in foster care at the age of two and was on his way to be reunited with his real mother. Oh, how sad. He was 10 years old and there was a terrible thunderstorm that may have caused the driver to swerve off the road."

"This is so cool," David said slowly. "I can't believe you really talked with someone who's dead."

Luke turned away from the terminal and stared out into space.

"Luke, are you OK?" asked Jennifer.

"I don't know," he replied. "I

have this strange feeling like I've relived the whole thing. Like it was partly me that died in that car wreck."

"Whoa, this is too much!" cried David as he paced back and forth. "Can you believe it? I can't believe it!"

"What'll we do now, Luke?" asked Jennifer.

Luke turned back toward Jennifer and sat down.

"I'm not sure," he replied in a quiet voice. "I can't even think straight. I just can't believe that there's a way to talk to someone after they're dead."

"Well, you saw it didn't you?" said David excitedly. "I mean, unless you're making this whole thing up.

How did you know that kid's name and everything?"

"I don't know. I just don't know."

Jennifer walked over to Luke and put her hand on his shoulder.

"Why don't we let someone else wear the ring and see if anything happens to them?" she said.

Luke looked up at Jennifer and narrowed his eyes.

"Well, I guess we could. Do you want to try it, Jennifer?"

Before she could reply, David stood between them.

"Hey, wait a minute," he said angrily. "Why not let me try it on."

"David we're not playing around," replied Luke. "Who knows what we've

stumbled onto? We could get into some
serious trouble."

"What do you mean? So you talked
with a dead person, so what?"

"Well, I didn't say anything
earlier."

Luke lifted his left hand and
showed them his bruise.

"This happened in the car wreck."

"No way," replied David. "You
must have fallen out of bed."

"I couldn't have. I was still in
bed when I woke up."

Jennifer walked over to Luke and
examined his hand.

"You say this happened in the car
wreck," she said nervously.

"Yeah, I was thrown against the
floor and landed on my hand as the car

rolled down the hill."

Jennifer took a deep breath and closed her eyes.

"I want to do it," she said. "Let me take the ring home and wear it to see if anything happens to me."

Luke took the ring out of his book bag and handed it to Jennifer.

"Are you sure?" he asked.

"Positive."

David started to mumble to himself and began to walk out of the microfilm room. Jennifer quickly gathered her things and walked up beside him.

"Listen David," she said as she put her arm around his shoulder. "We're not trying to exclude you. Just let me try the ring next and then I promise you'll get to wear it, OK?"

David took a deep breath and stopped walking.

"Well, I guess so," he replied. "But I'm definitely wearing the ring next."

"Definitely," replied Luke, who had collected his things and was now standing beside them. "We'll just see what, if anything, happens to Jennifer."

"Oh, great," replied Jennifer nervously. "I don't like the way that sounds."

Luke went over to the elevator and pushed the first-floor button. They all got in and silently watched as the elevator made its way to the ground floor. No one said a word as they walked out of the building and began to cross the campus to meet with Luke's dad. David finally broke the silence with a cough.

"What?" asked Jennifer as she turned toward David.

"Nothing," he replied. "Are you nervous?"

Jennifer slowly moved her finger against her chin. "Well, actually I am a little nervous," she replied.

Luke walked up beside her and patted her on the shoulder.

"You're our only hope Obi-Wan, help us."

"I'll do my best," she laughed.

Taking the ring out of her pocket, she put it on her finger and looked at David and Luke.

"Here goes nothing."

Chapter 4

Jennifer rolled over and reached for the dial of her radio. The music played quietly as her hand searched for the edge of the nightstand. Slowly, and a bit wearily, she opened her eyes.

"Where is that radio?" she mumbled. "They always play this elevator music late at night."

Suddenly, a sharp pain ran through her body. Jennifer took a deep breath and sat up in bed.

"Oh, what did I eat that would've caused that," she wondered as she rubbed her stomach.

In the background, her ear caught the sound of a radio announcer giving a special news bulletin.

"This is Ed Murrow reporting from London, June 2,1942."

"1942! They're playing a history program this late at night?"

Jennifer again reached over to turn the radio dial but felt another sharp pain. This time the pain was so strong that she grabbed the edge of the bed and held it tightly. Looking down at her hands, she saw the moonlight reflecting off the ring on her finger.

"The ring. I forgot about the ring. I don't think I'm ready for this."

She moved her right hand along the edge of the bed and could feel that the sheets were damp.

"I'm not going to let this happen," she said, clenching her teeth together. "I don't have to let this happen."

Jennifer tried to take the ring off her finger but her hand had become swollen. There was no way that she could get the ring past her knuckles. Feeling somewhat confused, she reached over to her nightstand and turned on a lamp. The sudden burst of light caused her to squint. Once her eyes had adjusted, she was surprised to find that her room looked strange. Her favorite chair that sat near the bed wasn't there anymore. The wallpaper that she had spent weeks shopping for with her mother was now different. Everything that was comfortable and safe was now gone.

"This isn't real," she said.

"This is all my imagination."

Her thoughts began to race.
Strange images and feelings rushed
through her mind. The image of a
pregnant woman and face after face of
different strangers kept appearing
before her eyes. She could hear their
voices and even smell the scent of
their clothes. She tried to clear her
thoughts by shaking her head but it
was no use.

"I'm in control. I'M in control."

Jennifer closed her eyes and tried
to calm herself. Thoughts of her
family warmed her like a blanket on a
cold winter's evening. Her mother,
her brother, her father; all gathered

around the Christmas tree. She could see them opening presents. Christmas carols drifted through her mind. She could almost taste the hot cocoa and smell the fresh baked cookies that her mother made at the holidays.

Feeling more at ease, she opened her eyes. The moment of calm was broken.

Her thoughts again began to fill with more images of the woman and her husband. She remembered details about their life together. She could see their wedding day, their honeymoon, and their house. It was as if the memories of the woman began to blend with her own. Jennifer even felt the woman's strong desire to have children.

Unsettled, she leaned over the edge of the bed and began to stand up. Her stomach muscles tightened as another sharp pain ran through her body. She tried getting out of bed but the pain was so severe that she fell onto the floor. Her arms shook as she tried to pull herself up but couldn't.

"You can make it," she said as anger filled her voice. "Don't let this ring take control."

Jennifer then clenched her right hand into a fist and slammed it against the floor. For an instant, she could see the room as she knew it - her furniture, her pictures, everything as it should be. She opened her eyes wider to get a better look. As she focused on the wallpaper, the images began to flow together. One moment she saw her cherished yellow roses and the next it looked as if they were soaked with a blood red color. One decade seemed to collapse upon another.

The images were so startling that she backed away from the wall. The last bit of energy left her body and she fell a few inches from the doorway.

Suddenly, the door opened and someone came into the room. Her eyes were unable to focus but she could hear the person speaking to her.

"I'm going to take you to the hospital," a man said as he picked her up in his arms. "Can you hear me?"

"Please... save my baby," she said in a whisper.

The words were coming out of her mouth, but she had no control over what was said. Before she could respond with her own thoughts, she lost consciousness.

A tingling sensation overcame her and she felt as if she was suspended in air. The tiny room grew smaller as she floated above it. Relieved that the pain had finally stopped, her body relaxed. Jennifer turned away from the sight of the room only to be confronted by the ghostly figure of a woman. The woman slowly walked toward her holding an empty blanket.

"Have you seen my baby?" the woman asked. "I can't find her."

"No, I haven't," Jennifer
stammered.

The woman turned around and began
to call out for someone.

"Allan," the woman cried. "I
can't find Allan!"

Jennifer didn't quite know what to
do. She didn't really know where she
was or what was happening. She
walked over to the woman and stood
beside her.

"Ma'am, who are you looking for?"
she asked.

"My husband," the woman replied.
"He's gone off to fight in the war and
he missed the birth of our baby. I
keep calling him, but he doesn't
answer."

The woman turned to face Jennifer.

She clung to the blanket as tears streamed down her face.

"Are you the woman I saw in my mind?" asked Jennifer.

The woman didn't say a word. She just stood there and nodded her head.

"Why did you appear in my thoughts?"

"I wanted you to help me find my baby," the woman replied. "It's been so very long and I haven't seen my baby. Do you know where my husband is? He could find our baby."

"I'm sorry, but I can't help you," Jennifer answered her. "I really don't know how to help you."

Jennifer walked over to touch the woman's shoulder, but she turned away. She watched as the woman walked into

the mist, calling her husband's name.
Jennifer looked down at her feet and
could see that the woman had dropped
something. She bent over, picked it
up, and examined it in her hand. It
was some sort of identification
bracelet.

"Ma'am," she called out. "You
dropped something."

The woman was too far in the
distance to hear her.

Jennifer again examined the
bracelet. The only thing she could
read clearly was the name Allan
Stepens. She felt sort of dizzy as
she tried to make out what was written
under his name. Without warning, she
found herself falling backwards into
the darkness. Farther and farther she

drifted. She couldn't sense the ground beneath her and was afraid to open her eyes.

Suddenly, she opened her eyes and saw that she was lying in bed. She stared in stunned silence at the ceiling above her.

"So this is what Luke was talking about," she said quietly. "This is just unbelievable! No dream could be this real."

Jennifer got up from bed and sat by her windowsill. She opened up the window and took a deep breath of fresh air. Quietly she looked out into the starry night.

"This is the last time I put this thing on," she said as she removed the ring from her finger.

Chapter 5

The next day at school, Jennifer walked into the building from the rear entrance. She hoped that David and Luke wouldn't see her as she made her way to the classroom. Slowly, she walked up the stairs to her first-period class.

"I don't want to talk to David in front of everybody in the building," she thought. "Maybe I'll get lucky and they'll wait until after school to bring it up."

Jennifer turned the corner of the hallway and looked into her classroom.

"Great. I got lucky. They're not here yet."

As she sighed with relief, she was

greeted from behind by David's hands around her shoulder.

"Did you have any bad dreams last night?" he laughed.

Luke popped his head around from the other side of her.

"Any that you want to talk about that is."

Jennifer was so startled that she dropped her books on the floor.

"You idiots. Don't ever walk up on me when I'm not looking."

"Touchy," replied Luke.

"Yeah," chimed David. "She definitely had a close encounter of the third kind."

"Ooh, you guys are such jerks. Let's talk about it after school, all right?"

Jennifer picked up her books and stormed off into the classroom.

"What's up with that?" asked David. "Is it my imagination or does she not want to talk to us?"

"Who knows? Maybe she had a bad experience."

"That's exactly why she should talk to us," replied David. "ET need to phone home."

"Would you stop with the movie talk, you really should read more."

Luke and David walked into the classroom and sat next to Jennifer. Luke was on her right side and David on her left.

"Look you guys, I'm not comfortable talking about this here, OK?"

"Why?" asked David. "What are you afraid of?"

"I don't want anyone to hear that we've talked with dead people."

Luke's eyes opened widely as he looked over Jennifer's shoulder.

"So you had an experience like mine then?" he asked.

"I knew it!" said David. "This ring is pure dynamite. What happened? I need details."

"Shut up David," replied Luke as he put his arm on Jennifer's desk. "Seriously Jennifer, what happened?"

Jennifer grew angrier at each question. Her eyes narrowed as she turned to face Luke.

"Do you guys not understand English? I don't want to talk about it now, OK?"

"But," replied David.

Jennifer then moved her eyes to her left. "That means you too, OK?"

"OK, OK," replied David. "We'll wait till later, ssh."

The classroom began to fill with students. Jennifer looked straight ahead to the doorway, ignoring both Luke and David. Just before their teacher walked through the door, Jennifer leaned over to Luke and whispered in his ear.

"I think it's time we paid Mr. Alexander a visit. I'll fill you in on my dream once we meet with him, OK?"

"OK," replied Luke. "We'll go to his shop after school."

The rest of the day seemed like an eternity to Luke and David. They were dying to find out what had happened to Jennifer. As soon as the last bell of the day rang, Luke and David quickly gathered up their books and walked over to Jennifer.

"Are you ready to go?" asked Luke.

Jennifer put the last book into her book bag and zipped it up.

"Yeah, I'm ready," she replied. "Just remember. Let's wait until we get away from the school to talk about what happened."

They all walked out of the building together and made their way to Mr. Alexander's store. The weather was warm and sunny, a perfect afternoon to be outside.

"Does anybody know how to get to his shop?" asked Jennifer.

"Yeah, it's right across the street from the city-county building downtown," replied David. "I went to his antique store one time while my mother was getting a copy of her birth certificate."

Luke took his backpack off his shoulder and stopped at a nearby water fountain. As he leaned over to take a drink, he looked at Jennifer.

"Was it as weird as my experience?" he asked.

"Let me put it this way," Jennifer replied. "This ring is trouble. It's almost impossible to control what happens to you. I mean, I tried to stop whatever it was that was happening and I couldn't."

"What happened?" asked David.

"You people need to give details."

Jennifer put her hands up to her chin and looked toward the sky.

"It was like I experienced this woman's life," she said. "I saw what she saw and I thought what she thought. I could even feel her emotions."

"Woo, that's so wild," said David. "What happened to her?"

"I think she must have died while she was giving birth. She said her husband was fighting in the war and she couldn't find him or her baby."

"You mean she spoke with you?" asked Luke.

"Yeah, she said she wanted me to

help her find them. It was so weird."

David and Jennifer each stood next to Luke and waited while he splashed some water on his face.

"Well, now that you've both had similar experiences, what do we do?" asked David.

"We'll get Mr.Alexander to explain what's happened to us, that's what we'll do," replied Luke. "After all, it's his ring that got us into all this."

For the next forty-five minutes they walked from the edge of Mulberry Grove to the center of town. Mr. Alexander's antique store was located in the oldest section of the town that was restored to look like it did when the city of Mulberry Grove was founded in 1890. The five blocks around the antique store were called the historic center. The streets were made of brick instead of blacktop and all of the old street lamps from the 19th century had been restored.

As they approached the elaborate stone steps in front of the antique store, David stopped the others with his hand and silently stood and stared at the building.

"This place is so cool," he said. "Don't you just feel the past staring you in the face."

"Control yourself David," replied Luke. "We don't want to freak Mr. Alexander out. It'll be bad enough to get him to believe us without your active imagination."

"Hello, reality check. It wasn't me who spoke to the dead."

"Yeah, you're right," replied Luke. "I guess it doesn't matter how you act. This is too bizarre to believe, anyway you look at it."

They walked up the steps into the building and asked to see Mr. Alexander. His secretary took them to the rear of the building where his office was located. Walking past row after row of antiques made Jennifer a little uneasy. She spotted a display of World War II memorabilia that reminded her of the identification bracelet that she had seen in her dream. A feeling of confusion and loss haunted her.

Mr. Alexander greeted them as they

walked into his office.

"Sit down, sit down," he said. "What an unexpected surprise. What brings you three here?"

They all sat down on a big sofa against the wall and watched as Mr. Alexander closed the door.

"Well," replied Jennifer. "Remember when you said that if we needed help to come see you?"

"Yes, I sure do," he replied.

"We need some help."

Mr. Alexander walked behind his desk and sat back in his chair.

"What can I help you with?"

No one quite knew where to start. Jennifer looked at Luke and David but they both shrugged their shoulders.

"Luke, you're better at

explanations," said Jennifer. "Why don't you tell him what's going on."

Luke took a deep breath and then began to tell Mr. Alexander the whole story. As Luke spoke, Mr. Alexander's eyes grew narrower. His chair swiveled back and forth as he tapped his fingers on the armrest.

"You see," began Luke. "This ring that you gave us, how can I say this, really works."

The room grew very quiet as Luke continued to speak. David and Jennifer focused their eyes on Mr. Alexander, watching the expression on his face. There was no reaction. He just sat calmly in his chair and watched Luke.

Once Luke had finished talking,

Mr. Alexander leaned forward in his chair and rested his arms on the desk.

"That's a very interesting story," he said. "You seem quite sincere. Is it possible that you two were dreaming? The mind is a very powerful thing you know. People sometimes swear they've seen things that just don't exist."

Luke got up from the couch and stood in front of Mr. Alexander's desk.

"I know it sounds crazy," he replied. "I'd never believe it myself if it hadn't happened to me. All I know is that something happened to Jennifer and me that was more than just a dream."

Mr. Alexander then got up from his

desk and walked over to his file cabinet. He pulled out a stack of photographs and began to examine them. One photograph in particular stood out.

"This is the photograph of the original ring," he said. "Now, how could a copy of this ring actually bring about your experiences?"

Luke, David, and Jennifer all crowded around the photograph. Mr. Alexander held a magnifying glass up to the photograph and examined it.

"Maybe a copy of the ring is just as good as the original," said David as he looked over Mr. Alexander's arm.

"Possibly," Mr. Alexander replied. "Maybe my friend, Jean, could find someone who has better knowledge about the ring than I do."

"Why don't you get the ring out of my pack so we can compare it to the photograph?" Luke asked David.

"Sure, why not, anything you say. I'm here to serve."

David sat back down on the couch and started to search through Luke's bag. When he opened the bag and saw the rings bright yellow stone staring back at him, he couldn't resist placing it on his finger.

"Well, all I know is that it's my turn to wear the ring."

Luke turned around and tried to grab the ring from David.

"Have you been listening to us?" he said. "We don't know what this ring is doing. It might be dangerous for you to be wearing it."

"Oh no," replied David. "A deal's
a deal. We agreed that I'd be the
next one to wear it and I'm going to
wear it."

Mr. Alexander walked over and
stood by David.

"Maybe that's not such a bad
idea," he replied.

"What?" asked Jennifer. "Do you
really think it's safe?"

"You say you were both asleep when
you encountered the spirits."

"Yeah," replied Luke. "I guess we
were asleep."

"Well then, maybe you two should
spend the night with David and see if
anything happens to him as he sleeps."

Jennifer and Luke looked at one

another and then at David.

"You just might be able to record something extraordinary."

Jennifer walked over to the couch and picked up her backpack.

"This was fun when it first started," she said, throwing the pack over her shoulder. "But I'm not so sure now. And I don't really want to see anything extraordinary, thank you."

David stopped her just as she was about to leave the room.

"Come on now," he said. "Why all of the sudden when it's my turn, you chicken out?"

"David, this is the unknown, spooksville," she replied. "This isn't some game. I don't want to be a part of it anymore."

Luke walked over to the doorway and held the door shut with his hand.

"I understand how you feel, Jennifer, I really do. But don't you think we should follow it through?"

Jennifer stood and stared into Luke's eyes. She could see that it meant a great deal to him. Slowly, she put down her bag and let out a sigh.

"If it means that much to you guys, I guess I can continue."

"Great," said David, as he turned to Mr. Alexander. "What do they need to do?"

Mr. Alexander walked over to the closet and took out a video camera. He set it on the desk and then put a pad of paper beside it.

"I want you to record anything that happens," he said. "Write down everything you see that's unusual or strange. Do you know how to use a video camera?"

"Yeah," replied Luke. "My dad has one."

"Splendid. It will come in handy in case you happen to see any...any...well, any spirits, shall we say."

Luke took the camera and paper and stuck them inside his backpack.

"I want you to call me on Monday and tell me what happened, all right? Sooner if it's really urgent."

Luke, David, and Jennifer shook their heads in agreement. As they walked down the hallway toward the exit, David turned toward Luke and Jennifer.

"Tomorrow night's Friday," he said. "You guys can come over and spend the night. Meet me at my house at 6 o'clock."

"Shouldn't we walk home with you?" asked Luke.

"No, I have to go to the dentist after school. Come over in the evening."

"Oh, by the way," said Luke. "Don't put the ring on until we get there, OK?"

David looked at the ring and then looked back at Luke.

"OK," he replied. "I won't wear it until you guys are with me."

Chapter 6

The weekend had finally come. Luke and Jennifer met at David's driveway and waited for him to return from the dentist.

"Do you think he's ready for this?" asked Jennifer as she sat down on the curb.

"Are you crazy?" replied Luke. "Of course he's not ready. I mean no one could really be ready for something like this."

Luke sat down next to Jennifer and began to rub a small stone against the pavement.

"I don't think Mr. Alexander really believes what we told him, do you?"

"Not really," replied Luke. "I don't blame him though, I wouldn't believe it either."

Jennifer rested her head on her knees and watched as Luke made a picture on the sidewalk. As she tilted her head to face Luke, her long brown hair almost touched the ground.

"So why are we doing this?" she asked. "If he doesn't believe us now, what makes you think he'll believe anything else that happens?"

"What do you mean?" replied Luke. "He'll have to believe us if we video it."

"Oh right, like you think a ghost would appear on video."

"Yeah, well, it's worth a try. Let's just see what happens to David."

Just then, David and his mother drove into the driveway. David quickly got out of the car and went over to Luke and Jennifer.

"What's up, guys?" he said. "Are you ready for the séance?"

David's mother walked up behind him and leaned over his shoulder.

"I hope you three aren't into any of that weird stuff that kids are into these days," she said.

"It's a joke, Ma," David replied. "I'm joking."

"All right," she said. "Just don't be up all night trying to think of any strange things to do."

Jennifer and Luke began to laugh.

"Are both David and Jennifer spending the night?" asked David's mother.

"Yeah, why?"

"Well, I need to know so that I can get the spare bedroom ready so that Jennifer will have a place to sleep."

"She can just sleep in my room in her sleeping bag, next to us."

"Oh no she can't. I'll put fresh sheets on the bed in the spare room."

"Parents," David said as he sat next to Luke. "She worries too much."

David waited until his mother had gone inside the house. As soon as she left, he grabbed Luke's bag and began to look through it.

"Do we have everything we need?" he asked.

"Yeah, I've got everything covered," replied Luke. "The only thing I'm not sure about is what we'll do when they see you."

"What do you mean?"

"They may want to keep you so they can study the habits of an idiot."

"Very funny."

Jennifer got up from the curb and brushed the dirt from her pants.

"Let's go inside and set everything up so we're ready," she said. "Besides, I'm hungry."

Once they got to David's bedroom, Luke took the video camera out and placed it on a tripod. Jennifer arranged her notebook and pens by David's bed, in case she needed to take notes.

"Let's go eat," said David. "We can hang out, watch a movie, and come back up here when we get tired."

"Sounds great to me," replied Jennifer. "I don't really want to spend the whole night in this little room."

"Me neither," said Luke. "I think we're as ready as we'll ever be."

As the night wore on, David grew more impatient. He barely ate anything and didn't really pay attention to the movie. Luke and Jennifer could tell that the only thing David wanted to do was go upstairs.

"It's past eleven o'clock," said Jennifer with a yawn. "Don't you think we should go to bed?"

David stood up quickly, dragging Luke with him.

"I get the hint, David," replied Luke. "Let's go upstairs."

David lead the other two up to his room.

"Don't worry about sleeping in the spare room," he said to Jennifer. "My mother's asleep and she'll never know. I'll mess up the bed in the other room, while you guys get everything prepared, O.K.?"

"Whatever," replied Jennifer. "Just don't get me in trouble."

Luke and Jennifer unrolled their sleeping bags and got ready to go to bed. David quickly returned, placed the ring on his finger, and sat on the edge of his bed.

"So tell me what happens first?
Do I see a bright light or anything?
Does my body start to feel funny?
Will I start to float?"

"Whoa, whoa, calm down," replied
Luke. "Nothing like that happens.
For me, everything seemed normal. One
minute I was riding in this car, and
before I knew it, the car crashed and
I sort of left my body but it wasn't
my body. I was inside someone else.
I experienced how this kid died."

"Yeah," replied Jennifer. "I was
me and I was someone else. I can't
explain it. I was thinking my
thoughts as well as someone else's.
It was so bizarre."

David was now too excited to
sleep. He got in his bed but he just

sat there and stared at Luke and Jennifer.

"Well, how should we do this?" asked Luke, turning toward Jennifer. "Do you want to take the first watch or do you want me to?"

"I'm kind of tired," Jennifer replied. "Why don't you watch him until two thirty and then wake me up and I'll take over."

"O.K., it's a deal. I'll watch first."

As Jennifer drifted to sleep, Luke and David quietly stared at one another. Neither one seemed to be tired. Luke, who sat at the foot of David's bed in a sleeping bag, aimed the video camera at David's head.

"Remember to get my good side on

tape," cracked David.

"You don't have a good side," replied Luke. "I guess I'll just have to video your feet."

After an hour and a half, both David and Luke were getting sleepy. David slowly reclined in his bed and drifted to sleep. Luke sat in the darkness and watched as both David and Jennifer slept. Images of the boy and the car crash kept appearing in his mind. He felt very alone. The dim shadows from the night-light next to David's bed seemed to come alive.

"Man, what am I doing here?" he thought.

Another hour and a half went by slowly. Luke got up every so often to walk around the room. He kept waiting to see some sign from David. Nothing happened. David didn't move a muscle. Noticing what time it was, Luke walked over to Jennifer and tried to wake her.

"Your turn," he said quietly as he rolled her over. "Time to get up."

Jennifer sluggishly got up and stretched her arms out and yawned.

"Have you seen anything?" she asked.

"Nothing," Luke replied. "Absolutely nothing. I'm telling you, I thought I would have noticed something by now. At least I thought he would toss and turn more."

"Great, we did all this just to watch him sleep," she replied.

Luke looked through the lens of

the video camera and checked to see if
the battery was low.

"Maybe you'll be the lucky one who
gets to video the after world," he
said, turning the camera off again.

"Just what I was waiting for."

Jennifer stood up and switched
places with Luke. As soon as his head
hit the pillow, Luke was sound asleep.
Jennifer sat motionless at the foot of
David's bed.

"I'm ready," Jennifer said
nervously. "Whatever happens, I'm
ready."

Morning finally crept upon
Jennifer as she walked past the
bedroom window for the umpteenth time.
She was never so glad to see a sunrise
in her life. David looked as if he

had never had a better night's sleep. He didn't make a sound the entire time Jennifer watched him.

"Luke," Jennifer whispered. "Get up. It's morning."

Jennifer went over and shook Luke until he was awake.

"Anything happen?" he asked, as he tried to open his eyes.

"Not a thing!" she replied angrily. "What a waste of time."

"Now wait a minute," said Luke, as he rose from his sleeping bag. "Let's wake him and see how he slept."

Luke got up and went over to David. He took his hand and began to tap David's face.

"Da-vid, wake up!" he said in a high voice.

David made a groan and rolled over in his bed.

"Come on, David. Wake up."

David took a deep breath and sat upright in his bed. He yawned for a moment, trying to focus on Luke.

"What happened?" asked Luke. "Did you have any dreams last night?"

"Yeah, I dreamed that I was late for school and when I got to class, I realized that I didn't have any pants on."

"That's it?" cried Jennifer as she stood beside Luke. "Nothing spooky."

"No, I guess not," replied David.

"What does that mean?" asked Jennifer, turning towards Luke. "Are we crazy?"

"I'm not sure what to think," he

replied. "I thought for sure something would happen to David. It doesn't make sense."

David got up from his bed and picked up the video camera.

"You mean we didn't get anything on video?"

"Yeah, I got a great picture of you rolling over in bed," replied Jennifer.

"That really stinks! Why am I the only one who doesn't get to talk with the dead?"

"Maybe they prefer intelligent people," replied Luke.

David walked over to Luke and began to shove him.

"I've had enough of your mouth. You think you're so great."

"Hey, watch who you shove around."

Jennifer stepped in between them.

"Stop it! Just cool down," she said, holding David back from Luke. "Don't say another word. Just sit down, both of you, and chill out. We have enough to think about without you two fighting."

David sat back on his bed and Luke walked over to the window. For the next few minutes, no one said a word. Jennifer left Luke and David alone as she went into the bathroom to brush her teeth.

"What'll we tell Mr. Alexander?" asked David.

"Let's wait until after school on Monday," he replied. "That'll give us more time to think. I'm not sure he'll ever believe us now."

Chapter 7

David got off the school bus and looked around for Luke and Jennifer. Not seeing them anywhere, he walked over to the playground and sat on a swing. The parking lot seemed quiet as he gently swung back and forth, watching for the next school bus. At first, he was relieved to have some time to himself. But the longer he sat, the angrier he became.

"Man, those two are always late. I bet they made the bus driver wait for them to get on."

In the distance, he could see another bus coming down the road that led to the parking lot. He got off the swing and waited for the bus to park. As he watched the kids climb down the stairs, one boy in particular stood out. The boy had a design on his shirt that caught David's attention. As the boy stepped off the bus, David walked closer to see what was written on his shirt. Before he could make it out, the boy's shirt changed colors. All of the sudden, the design was gone and the shirt had a number written across it. The boy's body seemed to stretch and twist, as if it was being reflected in a fun house mirror. David looked up at the boys' face and was shocked to see a man staring down at him. The man, who was wearing handcuffs, turned to face David as he walked away from the bus. David quickly rubbed his eyes and the man's body became distorted, changing back into a boy.

"Whoa, that was weird," he thought. "What was that about?"

Jennifer and Luke walked over to where David was standing.

"What cha looking at?" asked Jennifer.

David turned around and glared at her.

"Why don't you mind your own business?" he said angrily. "Why are you guys so late anyway?"

"What's up with you?" asked Luke. "Why are you so cranky?"

"Never mind," replied David. "Let's go inside."

As they walked inside, David turned around and looked back at the bus. For an instant, he saw the man with the handcuffs staring out the window. Their eyes connected and then the man vanished.

"That really creeps me out," he thought as he made his way into the building.

Monday mornings at school were always difficult for David. This Monday morning brought a surprise quiz. It was really a surprise to David, as he hadn't been keeping up with his reading.

"Man, why does she do this first thing on a Monday morning," he muttered under his breath.

David leaned across the aisle and whispered to Luke.

"Hey, man, would you let me look

at your paper?"

"What's the deal with 'man'?" Luke replied. "And no, you can't look at my paper. You should have read your assignment."

"Well piss off then, who needs you."

Luke was taken aback by David's tone of voice.

"What's wrong with you?"

David turned to face the front of the room and ignored Luke.

"Fine, don't tell me. Flunk for all I care."

David doodled on the edge of his desk as Mrs. Perry passed out the quiz. As she laid the paper on his desk, he looked up at her with hate in his eyes. Anger welled up inside him

until he was ready to burst. His hand
began to tremble from the rage he was
feeling inside. The rage lasted for a
moment and then disappeared.

"I don't care what happens," he
thought. "An 'F', big deal. These
people are losers anyway."

Luke watched as David drew
pictures on his paper. He wanted to
say something, but Mrs. Perry was only
a few feet away and would hear him.

As the day wore on, David appeared
to be more agitated. He kept playing
with the ring on his finger instead of
paying attention to what was happening
around him. Mrs. Perry called on him
to answer some questions, but each
time she did, he simply stared back at
her without saying a word and shrugged

his shoulders. David wasn't sure why he was so angry. He only knew that he was tired and bored and wanted to be alone.

Just before the day was over, Mrs. Perry set the graded quizzes on the edge of her desk and stood before the classroom.

"Who was the smart aleck who wrote the name 'Richard Long' on their quiz?" she asked, gazing at David, who wasn't paying attention.

She walked over to him and placed the paper on his desk.

"It seems that yours was the only paper missing, David. How do you explain that?"

David squinted his eyes and coldly looked up at her.

"What are you talking about?" he said. "I handed my paper in."

"Then you take responsibility for this," Mrs. Perry said, handing him the paper.

David barely glanced at the paper and tossed it on the floor.

"That's not my handwriting. I can't help it if you've lost my paper."

Jennifer and Luke were stunned. David wasn't the greatest student, but he never talked back to a teacher.

"If that's your attitude, then you can spend an hour of detention in the principal's office," replied Mrs. Perry. "I'm really disappointed in you, David. You're capable of so much more than this."

Mrs. Perry picked up the quiz and handed it back to David. Without even looking back at her, he grabbed the paper and walked out of the room. Just before he reached the doorway, he threw the quiz in the trash. Luke could see a big red 'F' on the top of the paper that was hanging from the edge of the wastebasket.

As soon as David had made it past the doorway, out of Mrs. Perry's sight, he leaned against the wall.

"Fantastic," he thought. "An 'F' and detention, all in one day."

David turned his head in the direction of the principal's office and saw a figure approaching in the distance. For a minute, he thought it was the principal, but as the figure

123

got closer, he saw it was the man with the handcuffs. He could hear his name echoing through the hallway.

"David. Da-vid," the voice whispered. "Set me free, David."

David was paralyzed with fear. As the man drew closer, he felt the urge to run but his feet wouldn't budge. The closer the man got, the faster he walked. He was almost on top of David.

"Hey," David yelled. "You're going to knock me over."

The man just smiled and kept walking toward him. David closed his eyes. The man kept whispering David's name.

"David," the man continued. "I'm going to take you over. Completely take you over."

David held his arms up to his face and closed his eyes. The man walked into David, vanishing into his body. David's body shook violently for a moment and then stopped. His eyes opened slowly as he took a deep breath.

"Ahh, to be free again. To be totally alive."

Instead of going to the principal's office, David briskly walked down the hallway and out the door.

At that moment, the bell rang. Luke and Jennifer walked out of Mrs. Perry's class and stood in the hallway.

"Wasn't that an interesting

class?" said Jennifer. "I can't believe David would be so rude to a teacher. It's not like him."

Luke and Jennifer slowly walked down the hallway.

"What's going on in his head?" Luke wondered out loud. "Is he crazy?"

"You don't suppose this is all because of the ring?" asked Jennifer.

"I don't know, but we're going to find out."

They walked down the hall to the principal's office. Luke popped his head into the doorway expecting to see David sitting in the detention chair. There was no sign of him. The only person in the room was the principal's secretary, Mrs. Atkins.

"Huh, isn't that weird," he said as he popped his head back out. "David's not in there."

"Oh, he must be," replied Jennifer.

Jennifer walked into the room and stood at Mrs. Atkins' desk.

"Pardon me," she said. "Did David Long leave detention yet?"

Without even bothering to look up at Jennifer, Mrs. Atkins replied, "Sorry, there's no one here by that name."

"Are you sure?" replied Jennifer. "Maybe you just don't recognize his name. He's average height, has brown hair, and he's very thin. Oh, and he was wearing a huge gold ring. Was anyone like that in here this afternoon?"

"I'm afraid I can't help you,"
Mrs. Atkins replied. "Maybe you
should try the nurse's station."

"No, he was supposed to come here.
Isn't that weird?"

"Isn't what weird?" replied Mrs.
Atkins.

"Oh, nothing. Sorry for bothering
you."

Jennifer looked confused as she
walked back into the hallway.

"Where is he?" asked Luke.

"I don't know," replied Jennifer.
"She said he wasn't in the principal's
office today."

"Well, let's get our books and go
out and find him."

Luke and Jennifer quickly gathered

their things and headed for Luke's house. As they made their way out of the building, they were amazed to find Mr. Alexander and another man standing in the parking lot.

"What are you doing here, Mr. Alexander?" asked Luke as he and Jennifer approached them.

"Luke and Jennifer, I'm glad we've found you. I'd like to introduce you to Mr. Lumore. He's the gentleman I told you about who works at the university. By the way, where's David?"

"That's a good question?" replied Jennifer. "He just ran out of class and disappeared."

"By any chance was he wearing the ring?"

"Yeah, he was," replied Luke. "Why?"

"Well, I'm afraid I've got some good news and some bad news. After you three visited my office the other day, I called Mr. Lumore and told him about your experiences. He asked me some questions about the ring and where I had it made. The good news is that you're not crazy. And I'll let Mr. Lumore tell you the bad news."

Mr. Lumore shook both Luke and Jennifer's hands and continued the story.

"You see, Jeff-a-Mr. Alexander, had that ring made for him when he was in Egypt. I did some research on the man that made the ring. It seems that his family is descended from a long

line of priests from ancient Egypt.
The practices of magic and
superstition have been passed down
from generation to generation. The
man who made that replica of the ring
still practices the ways of his
ancestors. In short, that ring is not
just a replica of the original. It's
an exact duplicate; magic and all."

Luke and Jennifer looked at one
another.

"We weren't crazy then!" replied
Luke.

"I don't think so," replied Mr.
Lumore. "I believe you really did
have encounters with the spirit
world."

"Whew!" replied Luke. "For a
while there I was really wondering."

"The bad news is that the ring could be very dangerous. The world of the spirits is very uncertain. Someone who is not experienced or prepared for it can really get burned."

"What'll we do now?" asked Jennifer. "David must have had something happen to him today. He wasn't himself."

"Why don't you two go out and find him and bring him to my office," replied Mr. Alexander. "Mr. Lumore and I have gathered some material that will help us determine what happened to you. Maybe we can find a way to explain all this."

"I have no idea where David is," replied Luke. "It's already afternoon and we may not see him until tomorrow at school."

"That's fine," replied Mr. Alexander. "Mr. Lumore and I will drop you off at home and then you two can bring David over to my store tomorrow after school, O. K.?"

"Great," replied Luke.

"I want you to call me tomorrow afternoon as soon as school's out."

"No problem," replied Luke.

Mr. Alexander and Mr. Lumore drove Luke and Jennifer to Luke's house. When they reached Luke's driveway, Luke and Jennifer both got out and thanked Mr. Alexander. As they walked up the driveway, they saw David crouched down behind a bush near the edge of the house at the far side of the driveway. David motioned them to come over.

"What's up with you?" asked Luke as he walked up to David. "Are you trying to get yourself expelled from school or what?"

"Let's go up to your room, I don't want to talk about this outside."

Jennifer looked at Luke and just shrugged. Neither one of them wanted to get into an argument with David so they walked inside Luke's house and went upstairs to his bedroom. Luke locked the door and both he and Jennifer sat on his bed as David stood in front of them.

"So, talk to us," said Luke. "What got you so upset today?"

"David is no longer my name, my

name is Richard. I've taken over the body of the person you call David."

Luke and Jennifer looked at one another in amazement.

"You're kidding, right?" asked Jennifer.

"No, I'm not. I've waited a long time to be free and NOW's my chance. I don't know where I've been, but I'm not going back."

"What do you mean?" asked Jennifer.

"One day I was alive, in my own house. The next thing I knew, I was trying to find my way through a dense fog. No people, no trees, no animals, no nothing. Just fog. It seemed like I've been wandering around forever, until your friend placed that ring on his hand. When he did, the fog lifted. I could see your world as if I were looking through your friend's eyes."

Jennifer got up from the bed and looked into David's eyes. It was though she was looking into the face of a stranger. She could tell that whoever was speaking, it wasn't David.

"So, you're telling us that David is trapped in another world?" asked Luke.

"Must be."

"But his body is right here," said Jennifer.

"His body's here, but his soul isn't."

Luke got up and stood beside Jennifer.

"What do you want from us?" he
asked.

"I want you to help me clear my
name."

"How?" asked Jennifer.

"I was once convicted of a crime
that I didn't commit. I could never
get anyone to believe I was innocent.
I want you to help me get a new trial
so that I can prove my case."

"What were you found guilty of?"
asked Jennifer.

"Murder."

Jennifer stood face to face with
David and looked straight into his
eyes.

"David, if you can hear me, you
don't have to let him take control.
You can will yourself back into your

body. Don't let him take control."

David backed away from Jennifer and put his hand on the doorknob.

"My name is Richard," he said as he closed his eyes. "David is gone."

Luke got up from the bed and pushed David away from the door.

"Your name is David. Remember who you are."

"Yes, your name is David," Jennifer repeated.

David held his hands up to his ears and tried to drown out the sound of their voices.

"David, can you hear us? This is Luke, remember?"

"Try to get the ring off his finger," said Jennifer. "Maybe that will bring him back."

"Great idea."

Luke tried to pull the ring off David's finger but David curled his hand up behind his back.

"David," said Jennifer. "Make yourself come back. Don't let him take over."

Just then, Luke and Jennifer heard David's voice calling out faintly.

"Luke, is that you? I can barely hear you. Where are you? I can't see a thing."

David's body began to tremble. The sound of his voice caused Richard to cry out, "No!" Without warning, David collapsed. Luke caught him in his arms just before he hit the floor.

"He's fainted," said Jennifer. "Quick, take the ring off his finger."

Luke grabbed the ring and laid him down gently beside his bed.

"This is too much," said Jennifer. "I don't want that ring near me anymore. Look at poor David. Do you think he'll be O.K.?"

"Let's hope so. I have no idea what'll happen when he wakes up."

After a few minutes, David opened his eyes and slowly sat up. Pale, and a little weak, he took a big breath of air and looked around the room.

"I don't feel very well," he said. "I think I'd like to go home and go to sleep."

"David, are you all right?" asked Jennifer. "Are you really David?"

"Yeah, it's me. I think."

Luke pulled David up from the

floor and helped him over to the bed.

"Do you remember what just happened?" asked Luke as he sat next to David.

"Well, I...yeah...that guy took over my body."

"You should be O.K. now, we took the ring off your finger."

David turned on his side and took another deep breath.

"I think I'm going to puke."

Jennifer and Luke pulled him up and carried him into the bathroom.

"I'm so glad we saw Mr. Alexander," said Luke. "Now that the ring is off his finger, maybe these weird things will stop happening. I'm so glad to know we didn't dream this stuff up with our imaginations."

"I wish we were dreaming," replied Jennifer. "Then this would all be over now."

"What are you talking about?" asked Luke. "Of course it's all over now. We just have to make sure that we don't ever put the ring back on, that's all."

"Why do I get the feeling it won't be that easy," replied Jennifer.

Chapter 8

David and Jennifer watched as the last group of students walked down the hallway. It had been a long day and both of them were anxious to go to Mr. Alexander's store. Luke, who was using a pay phone down the hall, asked them to wait while he called Mr. Alexander.

"Hasn't this been a crummy day?" asked David. "I've never had a day go so slowly."

"Yeah, and it's only going to get longer," replied Jennifer.

"What do you mean?"

"Well, we still have to go to Mr. Alexander's and find out about this ring. I just wish this were over."

Just then, David noticed Luke coming toward them.

"Was he there? Did he want us to come over?"

"Yeah," replied Luke. "He was there and he wants us to meet him and Mr. Lumore at his shop. They're all ready to see us."

"Great," said David as he closed his locker. "Let's get going."

As they walked to the parking lot, Jennifer suddenly stopped and began rummaging through her purse.

"I can't find it."

"Find what," replied Luke.

"My assignment sheet," she said as she checked her pants pocket. "I have to have it. Wait here, I'll be back in a minute."

"No, we'll come with you," replied Luke.

David rolled his eyes and sighed.

"Luke, you go with her. I'll wait for you guys here."

"If that's what you want, we'll be right back."

Luke and Jennifer went around the corner, leaving David alone in the quiet hallway. In an adjoining room to where David stood, a janitor was mopping the floor. As the janitor walked out of the room, David turned and smiled at him. The janitor nodded back and stopped to ring out his mop in a bucket of soapy water. David began to whistle to himself as the man cleaned the mop.

"Here late, aren't you son?" the man asked.

David slowly turned his eyes and politely responded. "Yeah, I guess so."

The man took out a handkerchief and began to wipe his forehead.

"Got a lot of cleaning to do tonight."

"Mm-hmm, sure looks like it," David replied nervously.

David grew very uncomfortable as the man stood next to him. Without saying a word, the man seemed to study David. His eyes looked David up and down, almost in judgment. The silence grew louder until David began to get fidgety. He turned to look at the man and, for a split second, thought that he had seen handcuffs on the man's hands. He looked again, but they were gone.

"O.K., that's it, time to leave," he thought.

David abruptly turned the corner and walked away. Not looking where he was going, he ran straight into Luke and Jennifer.

"Whoa, I told you we'd be quick," replied Jennifer. "Are you O.K.? You look upset."

"No, no I'm fine," he replied with a worried look on his face. "Let's just go."

Luke pointed to the hallway from which David had just come.

"You're going in the wrong direction," he said. "The exit is that way."

David looked at the ground trying to avoid eye contact with Luke.

"I wanna go out the door by the band room, in back," he replied, glancing sideways.

"Why?"

"I don't know, I just do." David stood quietly for a moment, buying time until he could think of a believable excuse. "Let's make it a race and see who gets to the parking lot first."

Luke didn't say a word. He folded his arms and stared into David's eyes.

"I'm not letting you by until you tell me what's wrong," he replied suspiciously. "You've got that 'I'm lying' look on your face."

David took a deep breath and visibly relaxed. He stood directly in front of Luke and put his arms on Luke's shoulder.

"Look, there's nothing wrong. I guess I'm still worn out from last night. You're right; it's much faster to go out your way. I don't know what I was thinking. Lead the way."

Luke motioned for David to walk in front of him. Jennifer and Luke followed as David went back around the corner where the janitor was still mopping the floor. Looking straight ahead, David quickly led them to the exit and out the door.

"What a relief," David thought as he walked past the janitor.

Once outside, David turned around

to say something to Jennifer and
noticed that the janitor was now
standing at the doorway, smiling.
David's face grew white as a sheet and
he began to breath heavily. He had
seen that smile before. The sight of
the janitor filled David with a
feeling of dread.

"What are you staring at?" asked
Jennifer.

She turned around and looked at
the doorway but no one was there.
Luke walked up to David and placed his
hand on David's shoulder.

"What is it?" Luke asked. "Is
something wrong?"

"No, let's get to Mr. Alexander's
place as quick as we can, O.K.?"

"Sure," replied Luke. "We're

ready when you are."

Luke turned David around and began to walk with him. Jennifer followed as they walked off the parking lot and headed downtown.

The walk to Mr. Alexander's was very quiet and very stressful. Each one of them was nervous and tired and emotionally worn out. David seemed preoccupied as they darted through the city traffic. Every time they needed to cross a street quickly or watch for lights to change, Luke and Jennifer had to make sure that David was paying attention.

Finally, they reached the city-county building across from Mr. Alexander's store. David stopped in front of the building and sat down on the steps to rest his feet.

"Come on, David," said Jennifer. "We can sit down in Mr. Alexander's office."

David didn't respond. He sat back on the sidewalk and closed his eyes.

"What are you doing?" asked Luke. "Get up, we've got to go."

Without opening his eyes, David took a deep breath. His body began to tremble violently as sweat dripped down his forehead. After a few seconds, his body calmed down. He then sat up, opened his eyes, and looked at Luke and Jennifer. Not sure what they had just seen, Luke and Jennifer approached him nervously.

"I want to go inside the building," he said. "Do they have

judges in there?"

"Yeah, they have a court room in there," replied Luke. "Why?"

"I must clear my name," he said. "Take me to see the judge."

"Are you crazy, David?" replied Jennifer. "Why do you want to see a judge?"

"My name is Richard, not David. I want a judge to publicly declare me not guilty."

Luke and Jennifer looked at one another and knew that they were in trouble. David's eyes were glazed over and his face looked pale. The same look they had seen the night before. Luke thought for a moment and then took Jennifer aside.

"You stay here with him. I'll go

in and talk with Mr. Alexander and see what he thinks we should do."

"Why me, why can't you stay with him and I go see Mr. Alexander," replied Jennifer.

"Because I thought of it first."

"Fine. You go and bring him back."

Luke and Jennifer both turned back toward David.

"Uh, Richard," said Luke. "I'm going to go over there, across the street, and talk to a lawyer about your case. I'll be back in a little while and tell you what he thinks you should do, O.K.?"

"I want to speak with him personally. I want to go with you."

"Sure. No problem," replied Luke.

"Let me talk to him first and then
I'll come and get you."

"I don't want to wait."

"Look, do you want our help or
not?" replied Luke. "Just let me do
it my way, O.K.?"

"Agreed."

Luke waved to Jennifer that he was
leaving and then crossed the street
and entered Mr. Alexander's building.
Once he was inside, he took a deep
breath and walked to the back of the
building. He knocked on the office
door and waited patiently for someone
to open it.

"Hello, come in," said Mr.
Alexander as he opened the door.
"Where is everybody?"

"They're across the street," Luke

155

replied. "Uh, they're waiting for me while I talk to you."

Luke took another deep breath to calm his nerves.

"I have to tell you, Mr. Alexander, Jennifer and David and I are in sort of a jam."

Mr. Alexander sat on the edge of his desk, beside Mr. Lumore, and crossed his arms.

"What kind of jam?" he replied.

"Well, let me start by saying that David also had an experience with the ring. His experience was a lot different from the ones that Jennifer and I had. Last Friday, when Jennifer and I spent the night with David, nothing happened. Or so we thought."

Luke stopped for a moment to

gather his thoughts. Mr. Alexander and Mr. Lumore sat silently with their attention focused solely on Luke.

Luke paced back and forth in front of the desk and then stopped in front of Mr. Lumore.

"You see," Luke continued. "Yesterday, we found out that David had been possessed by this guy called Richard. I don't know why or how, but it happened. We took the ring off David's hand and we thought he was back to normal, but today we found out that Richard hadn't really left his body."

"I felt this ring could be dangerous," replied Mr. Lumore.

"David is outside right now and this guy Richard is inside him and wants to talk to a judge because he wants to prove that he isn't a murderer. So, I came in here to see what you could do to help us."

"So, you're telling us that David didn't have a dream like you and Jennifer but he's actually become possessed by another person's spirit?"

"Yeah, that's right," replied Luke. "And this person, who says his name is Richard, wants to come over and speak to you. I told him you were a lawyer and that you could take him to see a judge about his murder conviction."

"Well, this is your ball park, Jean," replied Mr.Alexander. "You say David is no longer wearing the ring?"

"No, we took it off his finger

yesterday."

Mr. Alexander turned to Mr. Lumore. "What do you have to say, Jean?"

"From what I know, this ring was supposed to open a gateway between the living and the dead. There exists a dimension between this world and the next. Some people in this dimension are unable to cross over to the next world because of unfinished business they have in this world. From what you've told me, I assume this spirit named Richard was able to overcome your friend David's will and take possession of his body. The ring became irrelevant once Richard crossed over and realized that he could overcome David. You're going to have to convince Richard that he's finished his business in this world so that your friend David can return to his body."

"How do we do that?" asked Luke.

"We have to give him what he wants."

"You mean we have to go and find a judge and actually clear his name."

"No, we have to make him think that his name is cleared. If he believes it, then he'll release his hold on David and he'll be able to cross over to the next world."

For a moment, no one said a word. Luke just stared at Mr. Alexander.

"Jean," said Mr. Alexander. "I trust your knowledge on this. I'm willing to go along with this if you are."

"I'm game," replied Mr. Lumore. "I've never had any real experience with this kind of thing. My grandfather used to tell me stories about possessions so I know we have to be careful. Don't let this Richard spirit sense any fear or any sign that we're trying to scam him. He has to totally believe what we tell him."

"Well then, go out and get David and Jennifer," replied Mr. Alexander. "I'll pretend to be a judge, and Jean, you pretend to be a lawyer. We'll give it our best shot and see what happens."

Luke thanked them and left the room to get David and Jennifer. As soon as he left, Mr. Alexander set up

a hidden video camera to tape anything
that took place with David.   Now all
they had to do was wait.

Chapter 9

David sat in front of Mr. Alexander's desk while Luke and Jennifer stood behind him. Like an accused man, he nervously waited for Mr. Alexander to speak. Mr. Alexander reclined in his seat, signaling to Mr. Lumore that it was time to begin.

"Why have you come to this office?" Mr. Lumore asked David.

David leaned forward in his seat. "I've come here to ask for a review of my case."

"Could you please explain the facts of your case for us?"

"When I was twenty years old, I was accused of the crime of

involuntary manslaughter. I was the
driver of a car that was involved in a
wreck that took the life of a man in
his fifties. The police claimed that
my blood level showed that I had been
drinking heavily before I got in the
car. I didn't have an ounce of
liquor, not one drop. But because I
had a history of juvenile offenses, I
was an easy target. I swear, to this
day, that the breaks in my car went
out and I accidentally lost control of
my car. I wasn't drinking. Anyway, I
served my sentence and was released
from prison after ten years for good
behavior. I made plenty of mistakes
in my life but I was innocent this
time. I've spent the rest of my life
trying to get people to believe me."

Mr. Lumore stood before David, looking directly into his eyes.

"If a jury found you guilty, why should we believe you now."

"Because I'm telling you the truth. I couldn't afford a good lawyer and the lawyer I had didn't even care. He just let me fry."

Not knowing what to do next, Mr.Lumore looked over at Mr. Alexander for help.

"How is it that you say your over thirty and yet you look all of twelve years old?" asked Mr. Alexander.

"I can't really explain it. The last thing I remember, I was in my house, lying on the couch. I remember I fell asleep and when I woke up, all I could see was smoke. My cigarette must have caught the place on fire. I tried to reach the door but the smoke was so thick that I must've blacked out. The next thing I know, I'm walking in a fog and I can't get back to my house. I couldn't even see my hand in front of my face."

"So, how did you get here?" asked Mr. Alexander.

"Suddenly, the fog lifted and I see this kid. I don't know why but I kept following him. I just knew he was the way out. I just wanted to be out. I kept wishing I was and then all of the sudden I'm in his body and I feel free again. Next thing I know, I'm sittin' here talkin' to you."

Mr. Alexander was amazed at the expression on David's face. It was so

real, so determined. He felt
goosebumps on his arms as the impact
of what he was hearing hit him.

"Let me review your case in
private for a few minutes," he said.
"I'll come out and get you when I've
reached a decision, all right?"

"All right," replied David.

With that, David got up and went
out into the hallway. As he shut the
door, Jennifer and Luke turned to Mr.
Alexander and waited for him to speak.
They could tell by the look of
excitement on their faces that Mr.
Lumore and Mr. Alexander were
surprised by what Richard had said.

"It's important that we get him to
believe us," said Mr. Lumore. "We'll
wait a few minutes, then I'll go out

and bring him back. I can't believe
that this is really happening."

"Should I tell him that I'll
pardon him?" asked Mr. Alexander.

"Sounds good to me," replied Mr.
Lumore. "Just play it by ear. If he
doesn't seem pleased with that, ask
him what will make him happy."

After a few minutes passed, Mr.
Lumore opened the door and let David
back into the room. As he sat in the
chair, David seemed very tired. His
eyes were red and he was very, very
pale. Without warning, his body began
to shake.

"What's happening to him?" asked
Mr. Alexander as he got up from his
desk.

From somewhere above David's body

came the faint sound of a voice.

"Luke, can you hear me? I'm not gonna let him take control."

Mr. Alexander and Mr. Lumore both ducked their heads down.

"What on earth was that?" asked Mr. Alexander.

"It's David," replied Luke. "He must be trying to get his body back."

David then quickly stood up and looked around the room. He began to swing his arms in the air as if he was trying to repel something. The harder he swung, the angrier he got. He went around in circles until he finally stopped, exhausted.

"I won't let go!" Richard cried out. "Not until I get what I want."

For the next few minutes, David

closed his eyes and stood motionless at the front of Mr. Alexander's desk. Nobody approached him. No one was sure if he would become violent with either himself or anyone who was near him.

"His timing is incredibly bad," said Mr. Lumore.

"That's our David," replied Luke.

"If we can just get him to hold off for a few more minutes, Richard might leave voluntarily."

Luke looked over at Jennifer and motioned for her to walk over to him.

"Jen, talk to David and tell him to hold off. He might listen to you."

"You think so?" replied Jennifer. "He never usually listens to me."

"Try."

"O.K., I'll try."

Jennifer slowly walked over to David and leaned into his ear.

"David," she said nervously. "Don't try and fight him. Hold on for a few minutes. We'll help you back, don't worry. Just wait for us to call to you."

Jennifer backed away from David and watched to see his response. He stood frozen in the middle of the room.

Suddenly, David opened his eyes. He turned to face Mr. Alexander and Mr. Lumore.

"What is your decision?" he asked.

"We've decided to give you an official pardon," replied Mr. Alexander. "Your name has been cleared."

As soon as the words were spoken, David began to moan loudly. His body again started to tremble. It looked as though he was having a seizure as he fell to the ground with a violent jerking motion. After hitting his body against the floor several times, he finally stopped and laid quietly. He let out a large gasp, and as he did, the ghostly figure of a man stepped out of his body and disappeared. Battered and bruised, David sat up.

"What happened?" he asked. "I feel terrible."

Luke and Jennifer rushed over to him and helped him to the chair.

"Are you all right?" asked

Jennifer. "Are you hurt?"

"Well, I guess I'm O.K." he
replied. "At least I'm me again."

Mr. Alexander walked over to him
and put his arm on David's shoulder.

"That was something I'll never
forget."

"Me neither," replied David.
"Well, maybe I'd like to forget it."

"Well, you don't have to forget
it," said Mr. Alexander. "I've got it
all on tape."

Mr. Alexander walked over to his
video camera and hit the rewind
button. Nothing happened. He opened
the camera and was shocked to see that
the videotape had gotten tangled in
the machine.

"Oh, no!" he said. "Just look at

my tape! Now we'll never be able to closely examine what happened."

Secretly, David was relieved. For once, he didn't want to see any weird experiences.

"Do you think Richard is gone for good?" asked David.

"Well," replied Mr. Lumore. "I might know a way to find out."

"How?" asked Luke.

"There's an ancient method used by Egyptian priests to determine if someone has come in contact with the spirit world."

"What is it?" asked Jennifer.

"It's a special ointment that has to be applied to the arm of the person that is to be tested. I made some up from an old recipe that was handed

down from my great, great,
grandfather. It will tell us if the
spiritual connection is still open."

"How?" asked Luke.

"Well," replied Mr. Lumore, "we
let the ointment soak in for a minute.
If the spirit connection is still
open, a mark will appear on your arm."

"What kind of mark?" asked
Jennifer.

"It can be one of three marks.
There are three symbols that are
associated with this ring."

"Oh, you mean the heart, mind, and
spirit thing," replied Luke.

"You've heard of it?"

"I told them about the history of
the ring when I visited their class,"
replied Mr. Alexander.

"Great. Well, the three symbols can appear in different ways. They could appear in a group form, in a cluster of three, or they could appear in pairs, or they could appear individually."

"What's the difference?" asked David.

"The difference is that some people have all three things working in harmony, which is very powerful," replied Mr. Lumore. "Since it's quite rare for someone to be so in tune to their mind and body, the most likely thing that happens is that the symbols appear singly."

"I'm not sure why it matters how they appear?" replied Jennifer.

"You see, the symbol will tell you

what part of your mind and body connection is communicating to the spirits. It becomes sort of your calling card, or your spiritual name if you like."

"Whoa, this is over my head," replied David. "Let's just put the junk on and see if we have any."

Mr. Lumore gathered Luke, David, and Jennifer and sat them down on some chairs in front of him. He placed them next to one another, forming a straight line. Mr. Alexander grabbed the jar that contained the ointment. He held it in his right hand as, one by one, Mr. Lumore applied the ointment to their arms. Luke, David, and Jennifer sat nervously as they waited for the ointment to sink into their skin.

"In just a moment we'll be able to tell if your spiritual connections are still open, " replied Mr. Lumore.

A moment later, a deep red rash began to appear on each of their arms. David had the most deeply colored rash while Luke and Jennifer's were much lighter. About thirty seconds later, the faint outlines of what looked like small pictures began to emerge on their arms. As the images became clearer, one could recognize them as the symbols that were on the ring. They each had one symbol. Luke had the symbol for the mind, Jennifer had the symbol for the heart, and David had the symbol for the spirit.

Luke, David, and Jennifer examined

each other's arms carefully.

"What does this mean?" asked Luke. "We each have a symbol. We all must still have that connection you were talking about."

"That's right," replied Mr. Lumore. "It seems that each of you still has an active connection to the spirit world. Could I have the ring so that I can compare the symbols on your arms to the symbols on the ring?"

"Sure," replied Luke.

Luke dug around in his backpack and gave the ring to Mr. Lumore. Mr. Lumore took out a small eyepiece and began to closely examine the contents of the ring. As he was studying the ring, he noticed some writing on the inside of it that no one had noticed before.

"Well, I'll be," he said. "This explains a lot."

"What?" asked Mr. Alexander. "What do you see?"

Mr. Lumore took off his eyepiece and set it on the desk.

"It seems that whomever made this ring inscribed another message on the inside."

"What does it say?" asked Luke.

"It says 'May the lost souls find peace.' Which explains why you three only came in contact with spirits who had some kind of unfinished business when they died. The maker of this ring wanted the wearer to contact only those souls in need of rest. It was an ancient belief that the living

could aid the dead on their journey to
the next world. This ring was
intended to do just that. But there's
a catch."

"What kind of catch?" asked Luke.

"To really enable a spirit to find
rest, one would have to possess the
complete harmony of their mind, heart,
and spirit. Only all three, acting
together, would be powerful enough to
aid a lost spirit."

"So we really didn't help any of
the people we came in contact with?"
replied Luke.

"I'm afraid not. You see, it was
believed that of all of the parts of a
person, the spirit was the most
powerful. So, the symbol of the
spirit has the most power. If the

symbol of the spirit is not present, then you can't fully interact with the dead. That's why David was the only one of you to be possessed by a spirit. Only David could truly interact with the dead. Luke, your symbol, the mind, means that you connect to the spirit world with a caution. You don't quite want to give yourself completely so you stay back and analyze. And Jennifer, your symbol, the heart, means that you use your emotions to connect to the spirit world. You let your emotions take control and they could possibly get in the way, clouding your decisions."

"So we couldn't really help these souls, we can just see them?" asked Jennifer.

"The three of you individually could not help these spirits. Now if you each had all three symbols then, yes, you could fully connect with these souls."

"I think we're going to go home now," replied Jennifer. "This whole thing has been really interesting, but I'm worn out."

"Me too," said David. "My mind is so full, it's going to bust."

"Wait a minute," said Luke. "Will these connections we have to the spirit world stay open forever?"

"That I don't know," replied Mr. Lumore. "I'll have to do more research to find a way of closing them."

"Great!" replied Jennifer. "What

do we do in the meantime?"

"You stay in close contact with me and Mr. Alexander," replied Mr. Lumore. "We'll try and help you if you have any more experiences with the spirit world."

"More!" cried Jennifer. "I don't want anymore."

"Looks like you're stuck, sister," replied David.

Jennifer took her backpack and hit David in the back. "Only because I listened to you, you jerk."

Luke walked between David and Jennifer.

"Look, we're all three stuck with this now," he said. "Let's just try and deal with it. If we stick together, we'll be O.K."

"Why don't I take this ring and put it away," said Mr. Alexander. "Let's all go home and get some rest. Is it likely that they'll have more experiences, Jean?"

"It's possible but not likely," replied Mr. Lumore. "Just to be safe, you better put the ring away and definitely don't wear it."

Mr. Alexander took the ring and placed it back into the glass container that sat empty on his shelf. As he closed the door, he glanced over at it. He knew that sometime in the future he'd take that ring down once again. The final ray of twilight hit the ring as he pulled the door shut. The last thing he saw was a glimmer of yellow light reflect off the ring creating an eerie pattern against the wall.

"I have a feeling this isn't over," he said.

The End (for now).